RECKLESS

WILD IRISH #0.5

Vi Carter

Contents

Other Books by VI CARTER
<u>WILD IRISH SERIES</u>
FATHER (NOVELLA)
VICIOUS #1
RECKLESS #2
RUTHLESS #3
FEARLESS #4
HEARTLESS #5

<u>THE BOYNE CLUB</u>
DARK #1
DARKER # 2
DARKEST #3
PITCH BLACK #4

<u>THE OBSESSED DUET</u>
A DEADLY OBSESSION #1
A CRUEL CONFESSION #2

<u>YOUNG IRISH REBELS</u>
MAFIA PRINCE #1
MAFIA KING #2
MAFIA GAMES #3

MAFIA BOSS #4

MURPHY'S MAFIA MADE MEN
SINNER'S VOW #1
SAVAGE MARRIAGE #2

NEWSLETTER

JOIN MY NEWSLETTER AND NEVER MISS A NEW RELEASE OR GIVEAWAY.

HERE

CHAPTER ONE

FINN

"W HERE IS YOUR BROTHER?" My father bends over a map that takes up the top of the table. His index finger stops moving as I enter, but he doesn't look up at me. Shane stands firmly beside him, arms folded across his wide chest. I scratch my eyebrow in annoyance.

There is so much I want to say, like, 'Just because we're twins doesn't mean we keep tabs on each other.' Or 'Do I look like a fucking slave?' But our motto is carved into the wood that hangs over the dining table that is mostly used for meetings.

The Irish word *chlann* was carved into that piece of wood by our father's father, and it is carved into all of us. The family comes first, no matter what. My eyes flicker back to Shane, who still stares at me, a shadow of a grin on his face.

"Probably in bed with a whore," I rattle off, and that gets my father's attention. His finger slightly curls.

"Watch your mouth, Finn." He speaks but doesn't look at me. Is he fucking kidding? His mouth spews poison half the time.

I flicker a glance at Shane, expecting the grin to be visible, but it isn't. Instead, his head tilts slightly toward our father, his way of telling me to shut the fuck up and go get our brother.

"I'll get him now." With a sigh, I close the door behind me and take the stairs two at a time, slowing down once I reach the landing. I can hear the undercurrent of a beat. Darragh never switches his music off. In his life, the party never seems to stop. I can smell the cigarette smoke before I even open his door, and once I do, a lot of other smells follow.

Disgusting.

"Darragh, get up." I kick the base of the bed, where three sets of legs hang out. The alcohol fumes in the room have me wanting to open a window. My steel-toe boot connects with the bed frame again. A blonde pops up like a blow-up doll, mumbling as she looks around the room. Her eyes settle on me, and she slowly grins.

"Good morning." A polish accent or maybe Russian—I can't tell the difference—coats her words.

"Get out," I tell her. Her brows furrow as she looks down at sleeping beauty, who I'm tempted to kick the shit out of if he doesn't wake up soon. "Darragh, get the fuck up."

This time he does, and the second blow-up doll inflates. Topless. She does a double take at me and then Darragh. "Twins."

"You're a genius. Now get out," I say slowly for her. They both get out of the bed, and the second one yelps as Darragh lands a slap to her arse. I wonder sometimes how we're related. The idea that we shared the same womb is baffling.

"Da is waiting, Darragh, and he's pissed." I don't blatantly watch the girls as they get dressed, but I can't help the occasional glance; they are fit, a little too thin for my liking, but still nice. I light a fag as Darragh finally gets off the bed and pulls on a white T-shirt.

"Pick a different color," I tell him. I'm wearing a white T-shirt, and I'll be fucked if we are dressing the same.

"You know who you are like?" Darragh asks while pulling the T-shirt off. I don't acknowledge him but smoke my fag, hoping by the time I'm finished, Darragh will be ready. "You're like Da."

I snort because I'm the furthest from our father, and Darragh knows it. I don't respond as each girl moves past me and out the door. Darragh promises to ring them later, and they believe him. Our front door has become a rotating one with all of Darragh's women. None are ever brought back for seconds. He pulls on jeans, and I want to tell him to change them. I'm wearing jeans, but I don't want to sound whiny.

"What does he want?" Darragh slaps his face twice, and I'm glad that he shaves daily. I'm growing a beard just so we look different. Being identical twins is a pain in the ass.

"I don't know. Shane's with him," I say as I make our way downstairs and return to the dining room with my brother, like a good little doggy.

"Close the door," Dad barks, and Darragh does. Once we all stand around the map on the table, he finally looks up, blue eyes snapping from me to Darragh.

My father is a man that many admire.

For me, I hate him and love him. I hate how he sees me as someone to take care of Darragh. I hate how he treats Connor, my brother. I hate the control.

My mind moves back to the meeting as Shane kicks it off. "Land close by has come up for sale."

Normally, Shane doesn't speak unless father has asked him too, but I can see the irritation in our father's stance.

The smell of alcohol from Darragh is wafting through the room, and he looks like he smells. Bloodshot eyes blink several times as he slaps himself across the face again. If he keeps it up, he won't have to slap himself anymore; Dad is ready to flitter him.

Shane jabs a finger at a patch of green fields circled with a red marker on the map. "Over eleven acres has come up. Seven of it is bog land." We all stare at the green patch that Shane points at.

"Darragh, I want you to convince the new landowner to sell it to you," Father cuts in, and Darragh folds his arms across his chest while nodding.

"She's only just moved back here. She has no family or attachment to the land, so it should be an easy sell." Shane sits down at the table, his black shirt and slacks making him look like he's going to a funeral. Maybe he is.

"You go with him," my father says, cutting me with his sharp eye. Once again, I try to hide my irritation at being Darragh's babysitter.

"How much?" Darragh widens his eyes, and I wonder if he's high. I want to kick him and tell him to get his shit together.

"Offer her a hundred thousand."

Darragh nods.

"For *bog* land? That's worth like, what, two or three an acre? The good land no more than ten." I can't for a second understand why he's over paying.

"I didn't realize you were my financial adviser."

Darragh shifts beside me, and I clench my jaw. If Shane gave his opinion, it wouldn't be shot down, but the moment I do, I get a smart fucking answer.

"You both tidy yourselves up. You leave in an hour." My father dismisses us with a wave of his hand. I'm out of there and taking the stairs two at a time. My mind, for some reason, begins conjuring up images of Connor. It's weird how much you can miss a person. I hate him for abandoning me, but he has always been there for me. Now I feel so out of place in our dysfunctional family.

Slamming my door feels pretty juvenile, but I need to release some of my anger. I also need to get showered and ready to go purchase bog land.

Land that's only good for one thing.

Dumping bodies.

CHAPTER TWO

SIOBHAN

"*D*EATH. *IT COMES TO us all.*" That line is from Gladiator, one of my all-time favorite films, and it rings true to me. Right now, it's on a loop as I look down at my father. All the wasted time. All the what-ifs and whys. They no longer matter. All that matters is saying goodbye and hoping that the next time I meet him, we might spend some time together. I might actually get to know my father.

"Ah, Siobhan, I'm so sorry for your loss." Another farmer I don't know takes my hand in his. His other holds a hat that he takes from his balding head. His tweed jacket is worn and looks like if you'd slap it, dust mites would fill the air. But these are their Sunday clothes, their funeral clothes. Irish Farmers have their own unique style.

"Thank you..." I don't know his name, and there is a pause, like he's waiting for me to say it. His hand tightens on mine. "Michael." Another part of me wants to say Patrick, but I'm wrong either way.

"Peter."

I exhale a breath. "Ah, yeah, Peter."

"Peter, you're holding up the line." Olive, bless her heart, leans in across my shoulder. Peter is a big man, nearly seven feet tall, so being told off by a woman who is small and round is funny. But he moves along the line that just isn't stopping. The room is filled with men, mostly farmers, all chatting about how great my dad was.

My eyes flicker once again to his corpse. Each story I hear makes me wish I had known him. I don't feel sad or upset like any normal daughter would. No tears come. I even try to force them by thinking back to burying my mother when I was only fifteen. But I have nada.

The wake is to last three nights. Three long nights. Honestly, I don't understand why we have to wait so long, but it's a tradition, in case he wakes up. But my father isn't waking up. He's dead. For sure.

"Olive, I'm going to take a break." I need to get out of this room of strangers.

Olive nods sharply. "Don't you worry, Siobhan. I'll keep this show on the road." I suppress a smile that threatens to appear. She pats me three times on the arm. "You take a wee break. Come back when you're ready."

I don't delay. Instead, I move through the house quickly and out into the small backyard, which is walled in. I open the gate and move out into the farmyard. The large slatted shed that housed eighty cattle is now silent. It's an odd sound. Spending most of my childhood listening to the wails of the cattle, the silence is another reminder that everyone here is gone.

Swallowing the first sign of tears, I tighten my arms across my chest. It's freezing outside—my breaths form small white puffs in front of me. The light black dress isn't doing anything to fight off the cold. The wind prickles my skin, making me feel, and I allow it. Standing still with my eyes closed brings back so many memories.

My mother wasn't a conventional mother by any means. She would roll up her sleeves and come out to help Dad with the cattle. She would shovel dung, feed them silage. A pair of overalls was something she owned.

A small laugh bubbles from my lips, accompanied by my first cry. Dad loved her so much. I remember watching him watch her, hoping someone would look at me like that one day. But that was the before. Before she got cancer. Before everything changed and then he changed. Our home changed.

"Siobhan?" My name is spoken softly and like a question, which has me wiping my eyes quickly. Two young men—brothers—are standing in the yard. Neither are farmers, and they look out of place in my yard. Like when city slickers arrive and stumble upon our house, either looking to buy it or looking for directions.

The one who's closer has a soft smile on his face. His black suit fits him snuggly. His freshly shaven face gives him that city slick feel. Blond hair brushed to the side finishes off the look.

My eyes move to the brother who stands a few paces back. He doesn't wear black. His jeans and white T-shirt are finished off with a black suit jacket. His wild beard and wild blue eyes do funny things to my stomach. They're both attractive. *What an odd thing to think when my father is lying out a few feet away.*

"Yes, I'm Siobhan," I finally answer on an exhale.

"Darragh O'Reagan," the closest one says. "Knew your father. He was mighty." I take his large, and surprisingly soft, outstretched hand.

"Thank you." He's smiling too hard, and the smell of alcohol emitting off him has my eyes flickering to his brother.

"Sorry for your loss." His voice is deep, and I find myself nodding at him.

Darragh still holds my hand, and my eyes snap back to him. "We wanted to know if you had a minute for a chat."

It's my father's wake. But sure, why not?

"What about?" I remove my hand from his and take a step sideways just to put a bit of space between us. Folding my arms across my chest doesn't do anything to fight off the cold biting into me.

"We want to buy your land."

Anger I wasn't expecting ripples through me. I unfold my arms and refold them while shifting on my feet. I look at both brothers. Waiting for what?

I'm unsure. Darragh is still smiling while the other is looking around him, like he wants to find somewhere to hide. The fact that he reacts like that makes me like him a small bit more, yet these two brothers have arrived to my father's funeral to buy stupid land. I push down my anger, not wanting to create a stir.

"I'm not sure what I'm doing with it." There is a time and place for everything, and this isn't either. "Thank you for coming," I add while moving past both men before the second one with the beard stops me with his words.

"Your father was a good man." I look at him now. Really look at him, because he sounds so sincere, so honest.

"Was he?" I find myself questioning. I am sick of hearing what a good man he was. I want to scream that I don't know the man that was left after my mother died and took him with her, leaving behind a shell. Well, not a shell, apparently. Everyone else seems to think he was great.

His brows pull down, and I don't blame him. He's a stranger, and he doesn't need to know about our family problems.

"Sorry. Yeah, he was." I leave quickly and go back into the house. I don't go to the sitting room that my father is lying out in. Instead, I make my way into the kitchen that also holds a group of farmers eating sandwiches and drinking tea. A big pot of stew sits on the stove. The kitchen is warm and cozy after the cold outside. I settle into an armchair that faces the window and let the room warm me up.

"Siobhan, sweetheart, will you have a bowl of stew?" I smile at Teresa. She's a neighbor. Our home is down what is known as The Black Lane. It sits at the end by itself. Teresa is the closest, and her house is across the road from the lane. I don't know her, but when I got back, she was there taking over, and I didn't mind.

Everyone in the area is here to help, united in their love for my father. Teresa wears a woolly cream Aran jumper and has red rosy cheeks. Sleeves rolled up to her elbows couldn't cool her down. That wool is thick; I used to own a few of them. Once I moved to Dublin, I left it all behind. Just like the life I knew before.

Sandie settles at my feet—another thing I'm trying to adjust to. She is my father's sheepdog, one he got after I left. She follows me around like she knows I'm her owner's daughter. I'm not exactly an animal lover, and I don't want to get attached. I can't take a sheepdog back to my apartment in Dublin.

"I'm fine, Teresa," I tell her. My stomach grumbles, but the thought of eating makes my mouth water.

"Just a small bowl." She has kind gray eyes that smile, even when her lips don't.

"A small one then," I tell her, and her smile spreads fast across her face.

"A bowl over here wouldn't go astray," Peter speaks up from the group of farmers, and a few of them follow suit. Teresa is quick to dish out bowls of stew and smiles as they start to dig in. Compliments on the stew are passed around the kitchen, making Teresa's face redden and her laughter deepen, and it's in that moment I find this sense of peace. In my family's kitchen, surrounded by strangers, with a dog I don't own at my feet. The heat of the bowl is warming my hands, but the love of these people is going deeper.

Then silence descends on the room, and the shift is immediate. I look up to find the brothers standing in my doorway.

CHAPTER THREE

FINN

"HER FATHER'S *WAKE*?" I lean in toward Darragh the moment Siobhan is out of earshot. I feel shitty now. One thing I don't like is messing with the dead.

"Dad said she'd be vulnerable, make it an easy job." He stuffs his hands into his trouser pockets as we both watch Siobhan disappear inside.

"Clearly, Dad isn't always right," I say, and Darragh looks at me with a grin on his face.

"It ain't over yet, brother." He moves toward the house, and I follow quickly on his heels.

"You're not going in?" I ask, waiting for him to turn away from the house and toward the car, but no, instead, I follow him under the arch of the front door. This isn't right, but it'll be worse if I'm not there, just in case it gets out of hand. Darragh, on a good day, can't control his mouth. This morning, with so much alcohol still fueling his body, anything is liable to come out of his mouth.

I've been to lots of wakes, for lots of ages, and most daughters would be devastated about the death of a parent. Siobhan seemed lost in a way that I wanted to help her find whatever it was she was searching for. I scratch my eyebrow, not meeting the eye of the men who line the hall. Silence already fills the house, but a new silence follows us all the way into the kitchen, where we find Siobhan.

She's sitting in an armchair, a sheepdog at her feet. Its head lifts slightly as it takes me and Darragh in before settling back down between its paws. Siobhan holds a bowl of steaming food, and the look on her face appears to be contentment, which is unexpected compared to the girl I saw outside. The guilt that was gnawing at me lifts. The silence in the kitchen has her looking at us. Big brown eyes meet mine, and her nostrils flare slightly.

"Ah, Teresa, I'll have a bowl of stew there." I didn't think my brother would be able to stoop any lower, but yet, he does.

Teresa, who we all know as the area's gossip mill, takes a bowl and fills it for Darragh, who accepts it and manages to squeeze in on a bench with the other men. The only noise is of him eating, and I don't know whether to admire his brazenness or kick him.

"Would you like a bowl, Finn?" My attention is drawn to Teresa, and I shake my head.

"No, thank you." Scanning the room, I meet Siobhan's eye again. She has been watching me. Now that she has my attention, she lets the silky curtain of long black hair cover her face. My lips twitch but stop as Darragh starts talking.

"Teresa, you have a mighty pair of hands on you. Another bowl would be nice." He holds his bowl in the air, and Teresa looks like she might pour the stew on his head. That, I wouldn't stop. I move toward Siobhan, noticing the way her hands tighten on the bowl and spoon that she holds. It's the only tell that she knows I'm approaching. She looks so slight in the armchair. But outside, when she was standing in the yard, she was curvy and womanly.

The women Darragh brings home have that look in their eyes, like they've seen too much of the world. The bad part. But with Siobhan, there's an innocence I find myself drawn to.

I sit beside her and immediately rub the dog behind the ears. "What's her name?"

She turns her head while tucking her hair behind her ear, and up this close, I can see that she is indeed beautiful. Her lips are slightly red from the hot food—they're distracting—but what's captured me since I saw her in the yard are her eyes. Brown eyes that are deep and rich. Her eyes hold her emotions, and now, she's nervous.

"Sandie." Her pink tongue flicks out to lick her lips. I follow her movements.

"Beautiful," I find myself saying, mesmerized.

"Excuse me?" She seems surprised, and I stop looking at her lips and focus on her eyes instead. "Sandie. She's a beautiful sheepdog." She looks down at the dog as if it's her first time seeing it. My hand still rubs behind the dog's ears.

"Yeah, I suppose she is." From her face and tone, I can see she has no attachment to the dog. A part of her has no attachment to this moment.

"Jesus, Teresa, that is a mighty stew." I clench my jaw at how loud Darragh is being. He's normally a little more discreet. He must be still pretty hungover to not give a shit at a wake. I look cross at him, but Teresa is filling his bowl for the third time. At least that will keep him quiet.

"I'm sorry about him," I say to Siobhan.

She shakes her head slightly. "You are twins; not the same person."

"Yeah. Identical twins." I rhyme it off like I have a million times.

"Oh no, you are so different."

I'm smiling at her. "We are identical—same blond hair and blue eyes, same facial structure. It's the beard, isn't it?" I say in a joking manner. But she's shaking her head.

"You might both have blue eyes, but yours are different from his." Her words trail off like she might have said too much.

"How so?" I ask, wanting to know, like really know. Hearing someone see me and Darragh as different people makes my stomach tighten. It's all I've ever wanted to hear. With my family, they see us as one, and I hate it.

She frowns. "I don't know. You're different but the same." Her cheeks color, making her even more beautiful. "Now I sound silly." She sits up straighter, and I can see the strain on her face.

"No, you don't."

The conversation has picked back up in the room, but as Darragh stands, dragging his chair with such fucking disrespect that even I want to hit him, the room grows silent again.

"Teresa, you're a gem," he tells her, handing her his bowl like she's here to pick up after him. I can see the tightness around her eyes, but she just nods, taking the bowl from him. Each step Darragh takes toward Siobhan, I find myself leaning closer to her, wanting to protect her from him. He pulls up a small stool sitting in front of her.

"Me and Teresa go way back." He smiles at Siobhan—the smile that breaks so many hearts. I remove my hand from Sandie and sit straighter.

"I won't keep you, Siobhan, I can see you have your hands full." He waves around the room like she's having a fucking party. I can't stare at him any harder, yet his focus is solely on Siobhan. "I just want to make one final offer." He hands her a piece of paper from his pocket, something he must have prepared before we came here. Something I wasn't informed about. Siobhan reluctantly takes the piece of paper and opens it. I can see what's scrawled across it.

Darragh is smiling like he just won. "Now that's a mighty number, Siobhan."

I can see the side of her face, and it looks like she's holding her breath. Her delicate fingers move swiftly as she tears the piece of paper in two.

"No," she says, and I don't know why, but I'm so fucking proud.

CHAPTER FOUR

SIOBHAN

MY HEART IS RACING in my chest for more than one reason. My emotions were already a jumble before Finn and Darragh arrived, but now I feel like instead of walking, I'm crawling.

"I want you to leave," I find myself saying.

The room is deadly silent. Finn is the first to move. "Darragh, now," he says, his voice deeper. His words are quick, quiet—words his brother obeys.

Darragh gets up. He's no longer smiling, and a shiver snakes its way down my spine at how he looks at me. His eyes are hard and narrowed. He doesn't like being told no or what to do; that's obvious. But I'm not afraid of him, so I don't look away from his hard eyes.

"I'm sorry, Siobhan." I don't look at Finn as he speaks. I don't take my eyes from Darragh until he turns away. Finn walks behind him and leaves my kitchen. I can nearly tell once they've vacated the house as the noise level around us starts to rise again to normal conversation.

"Are you okay?" Teresa sits down where Finn had been sitting, and I find myself rubbing Sandie where he had.

"I'm not sure," I tell her honestly.

"They are bad news. Darragh is a pup." *Yeah, I can tell that already.* But she doesn't mention Finn. She's silent. I'm silent. I hate silence.

"What about Finn?" I ask stupidly, and Teresa is smiling.

"He's not the worst." I'm not sure how I feel about that. It's good because she says it softly, but 'not the worst' isn't the best.

"Yeah, well, they're gone," I say, wanting to wipe the smile from Teresa's face. I didn't want her getting any ideas.

"They'll be back. The O'Reagans don't give up that easy."

My pulse spikes, and I bite my lip to stop the smile which threatens to spread across my face. There's something seriously wrong with me that I'm happy about seeing Finn O'Reagan again. I get out of the chair feeling silly.

"I better go back in." Teresa is no longer smiling but squeezes my hand as I leave and take my place beside my father's coffin. Olive hasn't moved from where I left her, like she had promised, and I resume the senseless motion of shaking hands and making small talk while I listen to a room full of strangers talking about my dad.

My room is the same as it always was. Posters of Boyzone and Westlife are still on the wall. I'm shaking my head as I scan the room. The pine shelf over my bed holds a dozen books and a Mickey Mouse alarm clock I refused to get rid of. The bed is freshly made. The cream floral quilt cover isn't mine; it's from my parents' bed. Someone had pressed it, and the smell of the fabric softener has taken over my room. Sandie jumps up on the bed as I admire it.

"Just one night," I tell her firmly, and she lies down with her head between her paws.

But that's not what happens. One night turns into four. Sandie stays with me through the three nights that Dad is waked in the house and the night after I bury him. I still haven't cried, and each moment here in this place makes me feel more lost than I have ever felt before. Lost in a sense that I know this is where I came from, but I feel like I don't belong. I want to. The more I'm around these people, the more I want to fit in. In Dublin, it's a fight for yourself. It's a city and busy, and everyone is rushing with their heads down. But here, they look out for each other. They know each other. It's nice.

I wake up to an empty house and make myself a tea before sitting at the table. I miss the noise of the people. The tile floor is freezing, but the fluffy socks I put on help keep some of the cold away. I've switched my phone off since arriving here and know I have to turn it on soon and let my life come back in. I have so many decisions to make and a small amount of time to make them. Darragh's crazy offer plays around in my mind, but I did the right thing. He was being disrespectful, but on the other hand, that kind of money is life-changing.

I need a distraction, so I decide to finally turn on my phone. Immediately, it starts to bleep, and it doesn't stop as I top up my tea. Sitting back down, I scroll through messages from friends and work. I have only four more days of leave before I have to go back. My stomach tightens at the idea of returning to Dublin. A part of me doesn't want to, but I push the feeling aside.

Sandie's bark lifts me out of the chair as the house phone rings loudly. It feels out of place after the intense, empty silence in the house. I pick up the phone quickly.

"Hello."

"I'm looking for Siobhan Walsh." The man's voice is very formal, but I recognize it. I try to remember the name of the familiar voice.

"Speaking. How can I help you?"

"It's Brian Harris."

Ah, yes, that's how I knew him. He's my father's solicitor, the one who told me that my father had left everything to me. I was his only child, and with no other family and mother gone, I was the only option.

"Hi, Brian. How can I help you?" Sandie rubs against my bare leg like a cat would, and I shoo her away.

"We've run into a complication," he says, and I stop focusing on Sandie.

"What kind of complication?"

"Your father's sister is contesting the will."

I sigh. Great. Just what I need.

CHAPTER FIVE

FINN

DARRAGH TURNS AROUND IN his seat, looking through the back window. "Are we being chased?"

I lift my foot off the pedal, slowing the car down slightly. My hands sting from the grip I have on the steering wheel, so I loosen them.

"Finn, is there something you aren't telling me?" I glance at Darragh as he lights a fag in my new car.

"Don't smoke in here," I tell him, but he shrugs his shoulders while rolling down the window slightly.

"Oops," he says as he blows smoke out the window.

"You are so fucking disrespectful." I want to take my anger out on the pedal and slam it to the floor, but the winding roads won't allow it, and breaking every two seconds is taking the joy out of speeding. That's one of the downsides to where we live. The roads are only good for one car, and the bends are pretty severe. You can't open the car up here.

"I'll get your car valeted, okay?" Darragh blows smoke through the crack in the window again. It isn't just about the car. It's about Darragh being Darragh, and yeah, I also don't want smoking in my new S-Class Mercedes. She's my baby, and he's polluting her, and not just with his smoke. I've just picked him up from a house party and am taking him home. He had been drinking last night, and he still reeks of whiskey. His crumpled shirt and slacks are the result of falling out of bed.

"So now that we aren't going to crash, can you tell me what's going on?" Darragh flicks the cigarette out the window, and I can't stop my mind from wondering if it has hit the shiny silver exterior. Paying ninety thousand for a car isn't worth it when you have a brother who disrespects everything, including money. "You're not still mad over the chick with the land?"

Now I glance at Darragh, and he smirks.

"You know, her name is *Siobhan*, and yeah, I'm still pissed." He rolls his eyes at me before lowering himself in the seat and putting on sunglasses. The sun is hiding behind the clouds, but his headspace couldn't have been great. He looks like shit.

A moment of silence passes, and I slow down as we enter the small town of Kingscourt. It's dark and depressing—one long strip of shops that sells a little bit of everything, yet nothing at the same time.

"What did Da say?" Darragh sounds serious, but I can't tell for sure with the sunglasses on. I can never really tell with Darragh. He often smiles when he's serious and smiles when he isn't. Most people think that because we're twins, we finish each other's sentences. That makes me fucking laugh. I have no clue of what goes on in his screwed-up mind.

"That we should use scare tactics." My hands clench around the steering wheel again. The thought of doing that to Siobhan seems almost barbaric, and I'm lucky enough that I've talked him into letting me handle it, but once the funeral is over, that's my proposal. He surprised me by giving me a week to obtain the land.

"We should. She thinks she's playing smart, holding out for more money." Darragh slides out his phone and checks it before lifting himself up slightly and stuffing it back into his pocket. Irritation grows on me at Darragh's words.

"She was angry because you did it at her father's wake. Are you that thick, Darragh?"

"Let it all out, Finn."

It was all bottled up inside, ready to pour out of me. After we left Siobhan's house, I drove home and didn't speak to him for a few days. Every time I thought about his behavior at the wake, I wanted to find him and punch him. Each time I did see him, he was drinking, drunk, or with a woman. I told myself it was a sign to stay away from her.

"What you did was a dickhead move," I tell him, putting my foot down. We're on a straight road that leads toward our home.

"Are you going to start rooting and tipping at that?" he asks while lowering his glasses, and I want so very much to punch him in the face.

"I'm going to go like a normal person and make an offer on the land. I waited until today, when the funeral was over." I slow down as we approach our house. Most days, I don't notice it, but sometimes I can see how the house looks like a hotel. With twenty-four bedrooms, a gym, library, and even our own bar, it's a monster of a house, but it's home to us.

The sensor on one of the garage doors kicks in, and the door opens slowly. Four cars already take up most of the large space, but two spots are still available. I don't even have the car turned off when Darragh jumps out.

"Mind my fucking door," I say as he nearly connects with Shane's Audi.

"You need to get laid." Those are his departing words. I sit there, knowing that going inside and seeing if Dad or Shane are looking for me would be wise, but I restart the car and pull out of the garage, leaving Whitewood house in my rearview mirror.

I'm going to see Siobhan and convince her to sell the land.

CHAPTER SIX

SIOBHAN

"**S**ANDIE." I'VE BEEN CALLING her for the last ten minutes. Normally, she appears quickly, but right now, she's a no-show. It's not like her, and the worry I'm feeling makes me realize I'm getting way too attached to a dog I can't keep.

I return to the house and grab a woolly hat and my long black coat. It's freezing outside, and my Aran jumper, which normally fends off the cold, isn't working today. I hate that Sandie is missing, and also, talking to the solicitor and finding out my dad's eighty-year-old sister is contesting the will isn't helping my mood either. My father didn't speak to her, and I'd never met her, but my mother told me she was very wicked to my father and to the world.

"Sandie." I tuck my hands into my jacket pockets as I leave the front yard to check the lane. Turning the bend from my small farmhouse, I see someone bent down, petting Sandie. My stomach flips as Finn looks up. He's too far away to talk to unless we shout, but he gives me a wave, and I can't stop the smile that tugs at my lips or the butterflies that erupt in my stomach.

He rotates from looking at Sandie to me.

"Hi. I've been looking for her," I say as I finally reach them just as Sandie, the traitor, jumps up and starts licking Finn's face. He laughs, and heat rushes to my cheeks at the sound.

"She likes me," he declares, looking at me from under his lashes.

"She likes everyone." I say it without thinking, and Finn rises, still smiling, still causing my heart to pound.

"Does she now? And here I thought I was special."

A small laugh escapes my lips. "Sorry to disappoint you," I tell him. He's wearing jeans again but with a red jumper, and his gray jacket is open but the collar sits up. *He could model*, I tell myself.

"I was wondering if we could chat." The uncertainty in his voice has me agreeing. A part of me is wondering if he felt the pull that I feel toward him, but the more rational part of me is telling me this is about land.

"Let's go back to the house." He smiles with a nod, and Sandie follows us back.

"How have you been?" His question is sincere.

"Honestly, a little lost. I didn't know my dad," I tell him as we step into the house. "He was great when I was a kid, but... then my mum died." I remove the jacket, not looking at Finn. "Everything changed." I pull off the hat and try to compose myself as I turn to him. Finn has a way of making me say what I think. It's odd and refreshing.

"Woah." He moves back out of my personal space as my nose brushes his chest; he was standing that close.

"Sorry, I was just going to hang up my jacket." He holds his gray coat in his hand. The red jumper hugs him, and my stomach tightens again. He definitely works out.

"What happened to your mother?" We haven't moved. I look up at him, and his eyes stare at me intensely.

"Cancer. It was a long time ago. Sometimes it doesn't feel that long ago, though."

"I'm so sorry, Siobhan." His kindness is going to make me cry. I sidestep so he can hang up his coat.

"Thanks." I make my way into the kitchen, where Sandie lies in front of the fire, and put the water on the stove.

"Tea?" I ask as Finn enters behind me, making the room feel tiny with his presence.

He sits down across from me. "Yes, please."

I smile at him. "He has manners," I say jokingly.

"I make up for the lack of Darragh's." I can see the regret the moment he mentions his brother's name, and the relaxed atmosphere disappears.

"So you wanted to chat," I say, getting to it as I place a cup of tea in front of him. Milk and sugar were already set out on the table this morning.

He shifts in his seat while scratching his eyebrow. "About the land. I want you to reconsider the offer."

I take a sip of the tea. "To you, Finn, I would sell it." His blue eyes light up with surprise. I don't want the land. I have no intentions of farming it, so selling it is the only option, and to someone as nice as Finn seems like a good choice.

"Great." He smiles, but I don't.

"But I can't. An aunt has contested the will. Otherwise, it would be yours."

Finn seems quiet as he sips his tea. "Is she from the area?"

I'm shaking my head, but I can't stop the smile. "What are you going to do, send Darragh to talk to her?"

"No, I would talk to her."

"Finn, the charmer," I say, and my cheeks heat. Words jump from my mouth without my approval, but I like the spark they set off in Finn's eyes.

"You think I'm charming?" he asks, leaning in slightly.

I hug my cup closer to give my hands something to do. "I didn't say that. I said, *charmer*. There is a difference."

"There's that word again." He looks intense, and I find my own smile slipping.

"What word?" I'm starting to feel warm and want to take off the Aran jumper.

"Different. You said I was different from Darragh." He's so serious, like me saying it means more to him than he wants me to know, and I want to give him an honest and open answer.

"You have a stillness in you that he doesn't. You're like... a tree." It's coming out all wrong.

"A tree," he repeats, amusement in his voice.

"Yeah," I say on a small laugh. It sounds daft, even to my ears, but that's what he is. Strong and tall and sturdy, like a tree.

"I'll take it as a compliment," he says, and I pray for my cheeks to cool.

"It was." The room grows serious, and I wonder if I'm flirting with him without knowing. Is that possible? To be flirting subconsciously?

"I'm not very romantic, so I don't know what to compare you to."

"You think I'm being romantic by calling you a tree?" I drink my tea, but he can see the smile in my eyes. He's smiling again too, and it's doing crazy things to my stomach.

"I don't get out much," he says on a laugh.

"Me neither," I admit. Even in Dublin, all I did was work. I worked at Connelly's Hospital and took every shift I could, saving for a home. It's not important now, as I inherited one. I'm still not sure what do about the house. Selling it seems wrong, since I was raised here, but moving here isn't an option. I'm not going to commute such a long journey.

"Maybe we should go out sometime." His words pull me out of my thoughts.

"Yes," I answer way too quickly. My heart feels ready to explode. He just asked me out on a date, and I just accepted.

He takes a large drink from his cup before standing. "Perfect. I'll see you tonight, then."

I stumble after him, shocked at his words. *Tonight?* It seems too sudden; I don't feel ready. As he gets his coat on, I stand silent in turmoil, wondering if I should cancel.

"What should I wear?" *Nice, Siobhan. You don't sound desperate or anything.*

"I was thinking dinner," he says. I'm nodding because his jacket is on; there are no more distractions as he faces me. "Is eight okay?"

"Perfect," I tell him, and he grins.

"Perfect," he repeats before leaving.

Sandie appears at my leg, and I bend down to rub behind her ear. "I have a date with Finn O'Reagan," I tell her.

CHAPTER SEVEN

FINN

"He's not here?" I ask as Liam looks up from his laptop.

"He's out with Shane."

I want to get this over and done with. I've hated waiting to hear what his decision will be after finding out that Siobhan's aunt has contested the will. Liam is still looking at me.

He's the next in line once Father steps down. He never says much, but he's a dark horse in our family. His suits and slicked-back hair make people think his appearance means too much to him. But it's a control thing. I've never seen him lose control. His hair always sits perfectly, his skin is always clear, and his hands are always clean—to the naked eye only.

Liam isn't one for words, but he gets things done behind the scenes. He just doesn't like working with any of us.

I make a decision and close the door behind me. "I'm in a bit of a situation."

Liam sits back and joins his hands together on the table. The laptop is still open, a soft glow shining on his face. Sometimes he's like a fucking robot, and I falter, wondering if I should just wait for Shane and Dad to get back. At least they'll say it as it is.

"I have to get land signed over for Dad."

"I'm aware of that," Liam says while I pull out a chair and sit down.

"An aunt is contesting the will; otherwise, I would have bought it today. She's seventy and—"

Liam cuts me off with a quick wave of his hand. "You're giving the situation too much life. When something gets in your way, it's an object that needs to be removed. Not a he or she but an object."

So clinical. "Okay, so this *object*... What do I do?" I ask, hoping he has an answer for me.

"I don't know, but you have to consider the cost of moving the object. Will it disturb what it surrounds? Then you must deal with it at the lowest cost and with the lowest impact."

Great. That's some fucking riddle.

"Anyone know where Da is?" I don't look at Darragh as he enters the room; I focus on my fist resting on the table.

"He's out with Shane." Liam gives Darragh the same answer he's given me.

Darragh eyes me with a smirk. "Did I interrupt something here?"

"What, you've never seen us sit in the same room?" I ask him. His stupid grin and his stupid shirt irritate me. "What are you wearing?"

"This is my new lucky shirt." He's still smiling while he pulls out a chair. His shirt is bright yellow with palm trees on it.

"You look like a moron," I tell him, and he isn't fazed at all. Instead, he turns to Liam.

"So, stony, what have I missed?" He's the only one who can get away with giving Liam a nickname. Right now, Liam isn't smiling or showing any indication that he likes Darragh, but we all know he's the favorite brother.

"Finn has a problem with his most recent job. An aunt has contested the will, and he isn't sure what to do."

"I got this." Darragh cracks his knuckles while Liam looks at me. "Problem solved."

Problem solved? Problem fucking doubled. Send Darragh to do a job, and he creates a problem that I somehow become responsible for.

"No," I tell Darragh and get up.

"He is the lowest price tag," Liam reminds me.

"He's the highest."

"Why do I have a price on me?" Darragh asks.

Now, Liam looks intrigued. "This is personal?"

I want to hit Darragh as he smirks. "Yeah, he's banging the landowner."

"Shut up, Darragh. I just have a conscience." I can hear the half-truth in my answer. Yeah, I don't feel comfortable scaring a woman into stepping away. A man, I wouldn't think twice. But an old lady? That just doesn't feel right.

"And a dick." He's hooting with laughter at his own joke, and even though he's pissing me off, maybe letting him deal with the old woman would be for the best. That way, I would have clean hands.

"Fine, you do it," I tell him with a grin, and he narrows his eyes.

"Is this a trick?"

"Is it?" I ask him back, just to confuse the fuck out of him as I leave the room and start to get ready for my date.

CHAPTER EIGHT

SIOBHAN

S ANDIE BARKS AS A car pulls into the drive, and my stomach tightens. Standing up, I fix my red dress. It's tight fitted and goes to my knee, so I get that sexy-yet-not-too-revealing look. The doorbell makes my pulse spike, and with one deep breath, I open it.

Finn's eyes roam my body, and I feel each place they touch. I shift, unable to hold still, and his gaze snaps to mine. Closing the door behind him, I notice he's holding something.

"Wow, you are stunning," he says with a smile as he takes a bunch of roses from behind his back. He holds the bouquet out to me, and I take it and smell the flowers like they do in the movies. Now I know why women do that. It isn't because they care about the smell of the flowers, but because it gives them a moment to gather themselves.

I lift my head from the roses to find him still watching me.

"Thank you. You look great." His red, black, and gray striped shirt, along with a pair of black jeans, looks so good on him. "People will think we're trying to match," I add out of nerves, and he grins.

"People will think we're a couple." His lip tugs slightly, and I shift on my feet as his eyes darken.

My stomach tightens, and I give myself a moment to think about what it would be like to be a couple. My heart starts to race, so I push the thought away. "Let me just grab my bag and jacket." I bite my lip, trying to keep some of my emotions hidden, but from the smile on his face, I'm not doing a good job.

"We could always just stay here?" The boldness in his eyes has me laughing, but staying here sounds like the perfect idea.

"Finn O'Reagan, what do you take me for?"

His smile is gone. "It's not you. It's me. I'm not sure I'll be able to control myself."

And I'm laughing again. When I look at him, I suck in a large breath. He's looking at me in a way I've always hoped someone would look at me.

"What's wrong?" He's in my personal space now. "I'm sorry if I offended you." Stuffing his hands into his pockets, he ducks his head, looking at me with furrowed brows.

"No, you didn't do anything wrong." There's something that draws me in with Finn. I feel like I know him, like he sees me. I close the distance, and I can see the uncertainty in his eyes. He hasn't a clue what just happened.

"My parents loved each other so much. As a kid, when my father would look at my mother, I always hoped someone would look at me like that someday." My throat tightens from the emotion the memory evocates, surprising me.

Finn takes my face in his large hands. "Whoever gets you, Siobhan, will never stop looking at you." His eyes roam my face, and his thumb strokes away a stray falling tear. "Can I kiss you?" His breath brushes my lips, and my eyes flutter closed as my tongue flicks out and wets my lips in anticipation of the kiss.

"Yes." I whisper the single word, and his lips touch mine, and I'm on my toes, my fingers burying themselves into his hair before running along his beard. The bristle of hairs send electricity through my hands. His hands are still holding my face while his tongue flicks out and touches my lips.

Sucking in another deep breath from the sensation, I allow him entry into my mouth. I push my body harder against his, and I can feel the full length of him. He moves me carefully against the wall, one hand on my waist. But it's not enough for me, so I break the kiss. Both of us are breathless. I'm inhaling his cologne and that manly scent that has me squeezing my legs closer together.

"Too fast. I'm sorry." He's apologizing, but if he could see inside my head, he might think me very wicked.

I smile, taking his hand as I lead him to my bedroom. Flicking on the light, all my posters look bigger. I turn to him, and one side of his mouth tugs.

"Didn't take you for a Boyzone fan."

I don't release his hand as we look at the posters. "What kind of fan did you take me for?" I don't care about bands or music; all I want is Finn in my bed.

"Not sure, but not Boyzone. Maybe Steps?" he says. I'm laughing as I pull him to my bed, and his eyes narrow before they darken. "Are you trying to seduce me?"

I bite my lip as I sit him on my bed. "Would Finn O'Reagan like to be seduced?" I reach back and unzip my dress. I feel empowered when he swallows.

"Yes, please," he says as I let the dress slip to the ground.

I step out of it and kick it to the side. He reaches out, touching my bare thighs, and pulls me toward him. I sit on him, my hands around his neck. He's still fully clothed, his eyes roaming my face. I'm not normally this forward, but I know my time here is limited, and if I let this opportunity go, I would never forgive myself.

Finn pulls me into a kiss. I shimmy closer to him, and he moans as his bulge rubs against me. I sink deeper into the kiss, moving my hips, which causes our breathing to increase faster. I'm unsteady, wanting the fabric between us gone.

Sliding off his lap, I pull at his jeans, letting him know what I want. He stands up, stripping them off along with his boxers. His erection makes my heart pound. He doesn't unbutton his shirt but pulls it off over his head. He's perfect. His lean body is toned, but not too much. Gold hairs coat his chest, and I like it.

As we stare at each other, I reach back and remove my bra and then my underwear. I've never been naked like this in front of a guy, especially with the lights on. I'm more of a lights off kind of girl. But since opening the door and seeing how Finn looked at me, it made me feel not just beautiful but also empowered. I want to keep feeding the hunger inside him with each piece of my body.

"Sit down," I tell him, and he does slowly. He looks good naked on my bed. He helps me position himself at my opening, and when I sit down fully, we both gasp. All I can feel is him inside me, and it makes me grip his shoulders as I move up and down.

Staring into Finn's eyes, I see the ecstasy mirrored back at me. But behind it all, I see his vulnerability—the mark this world has left on him. Closing my eyes, I only allow the feel of Finn inside me to consume me as I move faster and faster. His pants and moans make me come fast, and he follows shortly after.

CHAPTER NINE

SIOBHAN

I'M LYING IN FINN'S arms, both of us still naked under the quilt. My fingers play with his chest hair as we chat. "That's a lot of brothers. Who's your favorite?" I ask.

"Connor." There's a sadness to his answer, and I look up at him. His eyes are half-closed, and his lips tug down slightly in the corners. I want to erase the look of sadness from his handsome face.

"You want to talk about it?" I kiss his shoulder.

"Connor gets overwhelmed with our family and likes to take a break every once in a while. I just miss him when he goes." His eyes look haunted, and I wonder why. But a part of me doesn't want to pry too much. I don't want to scare him away.

"Your family sounds intense."

"They can be."

"Any sisters?"

"My dad has been married three times, so we have one half brother and sister, and his second wife had a daughter from a previous marriage. But we don't see any of them." I nod. It sounds so nice to have such a big family.

"I wish I had siblings," I say honestly, and Finn kisses me on the forehead.

"Sometimes I wish I had none." We smile at each other just as Finn's phone rings. "Highway to Hell" blares in my room, and I raise both eyebrows in question.

"I took you for a Nokia ringtone kind of guy."

He scratches his eyebrow. "That's the ringtone I have assigned to my family members only." I'm laughing, and Finn lets the phone ring out. Pulling me against his body causes electricity to spark between us. I move my body over his and feel him come to life.

"I'm thinking we should skip the meal and just hang out here," I suggest seductively, and he laughs. "Our reservation was two hours ago, maybe more. So we have definitely skipped the meal." I kiss him just as "Highway to Hell" blares again.

Finn groans. "I have to get it," he tells me as he gets out of bed, and I admire his backside while he gets his phone out of his jeans pockets. I love how his bum is full and muscly but not too hard to touch.

Taking the phone, he goes out into the hallway, naked. His voice is low, but I can hear what's being said on his side. "What? I'm busy." The irritation in his voice makes me smile. "What has he done now?" Silence follows as the caller speaks. "I'll be there in twenty."

My heart deflates at his words. He's leaving. As he comes back into the bedroom, I try to pretend I wasn't just eavesdropping on his conversation. He picks up his boxers and puts them on. "Siobhan, I'm so sorry, but I have to go." I can hear the regret in his voice, but it doesn't stop my disappointment.

"Is everything okay?" I ask as he buttons his jeans. He pauses briefly and looks at me. I can see the turmoil in his eyes.

"Yeah, it's just Darragh being Darragh," he says. I want to ask why one of his brothers can't take care of it, but I bite my tongue. "I don't want to go." Pulling on his shirt, he sits back on the bed with a soft sigh and kisses me gently on the cheek.

"I don't want you to go either," I say, and he kisses my hand before getting up and putting on his socks and boots.

"I might get back, but give me your number, and I'll let you know." That makes me feel a bit better, so I rhyme my number off. I get one more kiss before Finn leaves.

The house is too quiet, and it's weird that I miss him already. What will I be like when I go back to Dublin? My stomach tightens at the thought. My phone beeps from the kitchen, so I get up and wrap myself in my dressing gown. Sandie opens one eye and looks at me from where she's lying in front of the fire. I refill her water dish before checking my phone.

I miss you already. I'm smiling at the message. The number is new, so I know it's Finn. He's too sweet. I save his number to my phone before I quickly fire a message back. *I miss you too. Hope you get to come back soon.*

CHAPTER TEN

FINN

I ARRIVE AT THE location that Liam gave me and park down a lane. He told me to go the rest of the way on foot. My stomach won't settle; I'm dreading what I'm going to find. Liam was brief, as usual, on the phone. He only said that Darragh's in trouble, and they need me. Darragh's always in trouble, but this feels different. Liam being present was the first thing that tipped me off. Then during the phone call, I could hear Shane in the background, so I knew this situation was serious.

I didn't put on a jacket, and the cold has me stuffing my hands into my pockets. The road is dark. Liam said to walk for five minutes, and on my left-hand side, I'd see a small bungalow. He was right. I stop at a bungalow, but no lights are on. The large black farm gate is half-open.

The gravel under my feet sounds too loud. No lights come on as I move closer to the gray dashed house. I opt to walk on the lawn; it'll be less noise. I take one small jump across the small hedge that acts as curbing around the lawn before I approach the side of the house. Liam materializes out from the wall and nearly gives me a fucking heart attack.

"Watch where you step." He turns, and I follow him into the house. We walk into the utility room that's neat and tidy—nothing out of the ordinary.

"What's going on, Liam?" I wish he would just tell me instead of playing the fucking silent game. But we step into the kitchen, and a small light in the corner allows me to see the scene before me.

My eyes snap from Liam to Shane to Darragh before settling on the body that we all stand around.

"What happened?" I ask, feeling sick. The woman isn't dead. She's like a fish out of water; her body is jerking as she tries to breathe. But it looks like her neck is broken, her face is covered in blood, and a pool of it is growing around her head.

No one answers me. Shane and Liam look down at her like someone spilled milk and they're wondering how to clean it up. On the other hand, Darragh is freaking out. On his haunches, he keeps glancing at the body and then shooting looks at all of us. A fag was burning away in his hand.

"What did you do?"

"She attacked me. I panicked." He stands up, his eyes wild. He's high.

"You fucking bashed her head in. Is this Siobhan's aunt?" I ask, but I know it is. My stomach twists. Oh, God, this was the last thing I wanted. Real fear crawls down my spine at the thought of Siobhan finding out.

"Man, she was crazy, scrapping me, telling me to get out." He babbles as if he's not hearing me, so I look to Liam.

"What do we do?" I ask.

Liam doesn't look away from the body. "Kill her and bury her."

I'm nodding, but inside I'm saying, No, this isn't right. Maybe we can help her.

I run my hands through my hair and step away from this madness. "Or we could ring an ambulance." I know that's not going to happen, but for Siobhan, I feel I should try.

"I'll get the stuff out of my car," Shane says, ignoring my comment, and Liam nods at him.

"Pick up the cigarette butt," Liam tells Darragh, who's lighting up another one.

"Are you fucking stupid? They'll take your DNA off that," I growl. I want to strangle him as I pick up the butt and take the fag out of his mouth. I run it under the tap, then put both into my pocket.

The woman is still twitching, and I want someone to put her out of her misery. Rubbing my face, I turn away from the scene again, hating what my family can do to another human being.

"I'm sorry, Finn." Darragh is beside me. The smell of drink emanating off him has me closing my eyes. "I fucked up."

He's nearly crying, and I hate that. I hate what he's done, but I don't like to see him hurting either. I know behind all this, he's a good person.

"It's fine, Darragh. Just try not to touch anything," I tell him as Shane arrives. I notice that Liam has been watching us with interest, but he says nothing while he helps Shane lay down heavy plastic.

"Grab her legs," Shane tells me, and I do as he asks as he takes the top part of her body. I try not to think about the flesh in my hands. I try not to think about the fact that I'm helping to kill someone.

I try to just do as my brother asks and not think too much about it. We lift her onto the plastic. We've just laid her down when Liam kneels in a suit and covers her mouth with a cloth. I can't take my eyes off her—she twitches and fights, but she has no chance. I wait until her body stops jerking before I look away.

"Is she dead?" Darragh asks, kneeling down again and staring at her. Having him here is pointless.

"Shane and I will bury her and clean up here. You take Darragh home, and in the morning, call the Gardaí and report his car stolen. We'll burn it." I'm nodding, feeling a sense of relief at getting out of here.

"Darragh." Liam says his name harsher then I've ever heard, and we all stop and wait for him to speak again. "You were partying all night." Darragh nods. "Burn your clothes too."

"We will," I tell Liam. I just want to get away from here.

"I'm sorry," Darragh pleads with Liam, but he's already rolling up the body. I take Darragh by the arm and out of the house.

***

I'm staring into the fire as the last fibers of our clothes go up. Darragh's asleep in bed. Tomorrow, this will all feel like a bad dream to him. For me, it's a waking nightmare. My phone sits on the mantelpiece as I poke the fire while drinking straight from a bottle of whiskey.

I want to ring Siobhan, and I want to ring Connor, but I don't for two different reasons. With Siobhan, it's the guilt of knowing what I know. Knowing that my family is responsible for her aunt's death. With Connor, I feel that hearing his voice will push me over the edge. He's the one who beat up the bullies in school. He's the one who dusted off my clothes when I fell.

He told me I was a good person, worthy of a happily ever after. He told me I would always have him, but as we grew up, he disappeared more and more.

"Finn." I turn as my father enters the empty room. Once, it was a ballroom, but now it's empty. I chose this room so no one would come near me.

My father stands near the fireplace, his head held high. He isn't looking at me.

"What you did today for your brother… He will always be grateful." *Well, that's a load of horse shit*, but I nod my head like I agree. "You don't believe me?" The question surprises me. He never asks my opinion or thoughts on things.

"No. I don't," I tell him honestly. "He will do it again because, like all things with Darragh, there are no consequences. You taught us that sometimes blood has to be taken, but never from an innocent or a woman."

Father nods his acknowledgment at that statement, and lines appear on his forehead like he's really thinking. "But how many times has he broken that rule? How much more blood will he spill before he's caught? Or worse, someone else gets to him first."

My father nods again before he starts to speak. I fold my arms across my chest, trying to push down the anger that's growing inside me.

"When I was a kid, my brother and I were playing in a farm shed along with the farmer's son."

I'm glued to each word. Him talking about his childhood rarely happens, but hearing about his past makes my father seem more human. Maybe that's why he never speaks of it. I unfold my arms now and stuff my hands into my pockets.

"The farmer had left a double barrel shotgun lying around. He went out that day to shoot crows that had been picking holes in his cover for the silage, but by tea time, none had arrived. So he left the gun in the shed. Loaded."

Father unbuttons his suit jacket, like a man who's getting ready to sit down, yet he stays standing.

The door opens, and Shane looks in. Once again, Shane is dressed in all black. His dark brown eyes remind me of trying to see the bottom of a well, and you're just not sure you're seeing the end.

"Come in, Shane. I'm just telling Finn a story." Shane doesn't blink. He comes in and stands around the dwindling fire, looking from me to Father, but he doesn't speak. Father waits until the room settles again. I want to ask Shane if it's done—is the body gone? But I know better than to interrupt our father.

"The farmer's son, Patrick, was my and Tom's best friend. Anyway, Tom found the gun and was playing with it. We didn't know it was loaded, but Patrick told him to stop waving the gun around. When Tom went to lower it, he hit the trigger by accident and blew a hole in Patrick. It was a mess; we were only sixteen. He was dead within minutes. He was innocent. It was an accident. But I knew no one would believe us. Everyone saw my brother as someone evil. He liked to torture small animals, but that didn't make him a serial killer."

My father's gaze falls on the bottle of whiskey. "Give me that," he says, and it takes me a second to realize he's talking about the bottle.

I hand it over, and he takes a deep swallow. I want to ask what happened, but Father hands me the bottle. I take a quick drink, letting some of it drip down my chin before handing it to Shane, who declines and places it back on the fireplace.

"So we dragged him over to the silage pit and placed him slightly under the cover. We washed away the blood and spread fresh straw, burned the bloodied ones, and wiped down the gun before placing it where we had found it."

I feel sick at his story. But covering up a crime at the age of sixteen does explain how my father can now do it so easily, and like with everything this family does, he justifies it.

Father indicates to Shane to pass him the whiskey again, and Shane does. The bottle goes around again. Shane drinks this time, and from the look on his face, this is his first time hearing this story too.

"When all was said and done, the farmer had a drinking problem, so he thought he had done it. That bit of information we actually hadn't known. It was pure luck. But me and Tom walked away from it all. The farmer, however, went down for ten years. Wasn't really that long of a sentence."

This time, I take the whiskey. That wasn't the end I was expecting. The man served time for a crime he didn't commit. But it wasn't that part that messed me up; it was living with the knowledge that he had killed his son when he hadn't. There might be a wife or other siblings that would think their dad took their brother's life.

"The reason, Finn, I am telling you this is because Tom is like Darragh, and just like I stood beside Tom, you stood beside Darragh. Right now, he might not appreciate it, but one day he will." He squeezes my shoulder as he goes to leave the room.

"Did Tom appreciate what you did?" I ask.

"Yes." Father sounds distant, and I want to see his face, but his back is still to me.

"Why have I never heard of Tom?"

When my father turns around, his eyes have hardened. "That's a story for another day."

I'm left with Shane now, and I honestly don't want to be alone in his presence. He unsettles me in a way I can't explain, but I want to ask about Siobhan's aunt.

"So you and Liam finished that," I say and he nods. "Where?" I ask, and he folds his arms across his chest.

His tattooed arm is a reminder of why I don't like being around him. He has twelve black bands now that are thickly inked. Each time I see a new one, my stomach heaves, and I find it hard to hold eye contact with him. Each band is for a life that he took.

"Do you really want to know?" he asks.

"I'm off to bed," I tell him. I don't want to know. He's staring into the glow of the fire. I take my phone off the mantelpiece and leave the room that will forever remind me of a woman we killed, and Patrick. This house is filling with ghosts, fast.

CHAPTER ELEVEN

SIOBHAN

IT'S ODD. THE SMELL of the farmyard is giving me peace. Whereas before, If I ever got a hint of farmland in Dublin, it used to remind me of home, and that would put me in a foul humor. But now it smells like freedom. Hope. It's filled with memories.

I wish I had known my father. I wish I had grown up here and known Finn. I know I'm only twenty-six, but already, I feel as though I wasted years not knowing him. How can I feel this way about someone who I've just met? I'm smiling as Sandie follows me around the yard.

I'm wearing my Da's size ten wellies, so I'm swimming in them. But I don't care. I want this to become a memory—a little girl who wore her daddy's wellies out into the farmyard.

"You look good." Finn's voice sends butterflies erupting in my stomach. It takes all my will not to look at him. After not coming back to me last night, I do feel a bit of punishment is due. So I keep walking slowly, but I can't not look and find myself taking quick glances at him, sending my heart pounding.

"So this is what you country boys are into?" I tease, and Finn smiles, walking with me but not beside me.

"I like the boots and all, but it depends on who's standing in them."

I stop walking and smile at him. "Is that so?" He's freshly showered. His blond hair is still damp. The red T-shirt and jeans hug his slim body, and I let myself admire it for a moment.

"You can leave them on if you want to," he says, taking a step toward me.

"They're my dad's," I say honestly, and the horror on his face has me laughing.

"I'm so sorry, Siobhan." I can hear him, but the laughter isn't easing up, and soon he joins me. Sandie starts to whine, and I pull myself together.

"Not exactly sure why that was so funny," I tell him, and he nudges me.

"I'm sorry for not coming back last night. Did you get my text?"

I did. He apologized, saying Darragh had gotten sick everywhere, and he was covered in it. He had to shower, and it was way too late to come back. But still, I felt disappointed and hurt. The idea of Darragh always coming first didn't sit well with me.

"I did." I kick a pebble with my huge boots and watch it roll toward a slurry pit.

"I got you something." Finn sounds nervous, and that's what makes me look at him more than the box he holds out to me.

I take it slowly, looking from the box to him. "You didn't have to," I tell him.

"Open it." He's smiling, and I open it to see a gorgeous slim bracelet. Finn removes it from the box and puts it on my wrist. "Do you like it?"

My throat closes as I move my wrist, the light catching it.

"It's beautiful, Finn." I'm looking from him to the bracelet. It's perfect and he's perfect. This moment is perfect, and it's making my throat tighten.

"Why do you look so sad?" He lifts my chin, making me look at him.

"I'm not staying, Finn." I whisper the words that have lodged themselves in my throat, not wanting to come out.

"Staying here?" he questions, and I nod.

"I have to go back to Dublin tomorrow—to my job, to my life." *What life?* An empty apartment. Twelve hour shifts at the hospital. For the first time, I feel like I'm living. But I can't run away again. I did it once and swore I would never run again.

I want to remove the bracelet because now it doesn't feel right, but he stops me. I've never seen his face so serious.

"I got it with you in mind. It's yours, no matter what."

My throat burns, and I have to look away. I hate the silence.

"Maybe a cup of tea would be nice?" I ask, and when I look at him, he finally smiles again. It's not one of his full-on smiles, but I'll take it.

"Is that code for something else?" he asks, and just like that, the tension is lifted, and I laugh and try to look sexy as I shuffle in my dad's wellies back into the house.

I'm through the back door when his arms wrap around me, stopping me in the tracks. Sandie zooms past us and goes to her usual spot beside the fire. I'm lifted slowly out of the wellies, and Finn doesn't put me down until we're standing in the kitchen. His breath is hot on my neck, and I close my eyes and inhale him.

As he spins me around, I wrap my arms around his neck. I look into his heavy blue eyes, and I feel so much is said between us. This isn't love; it's not there yet. But it's so close that it's scary when I think of it. Once again, I don't want to go back to Dublin, not when I have so much standing in front of me.

"I'm taking the lead," Finn informs me, and I don't disagree.

CHAPTER TWELVE

SIOBHAN

T HIS TIME, IT'S *MY* phone that keeps ringing. I'm so cozy in bed with Finn, and I don't want to come back to the real world. He pulls the blankets off my head; I've been hiding out down here, lying on his chest of manly hair as I just enjoy the feel of him under me. The smell of him surrounds me, and I'm pretending that this is normal. That this is mine forever.

"Your phone is ringing," he says with a smirk, and I know I should answer it.

"Fine," I mumble and reluctantly get out of bed. Throwing on my dressing gown, I make my way to the kitchen, where I left my phone. Each step away from Finn makes me want to run back to bed and curl up with him. I need to get a grip on myself. I'm leaving tomorrow. That thought fills me with dread. I reach for the phone, wanting to stop my thoughts. "Hello."

"Siobhan, it's Brian Harris."

I sit down, waiting for what could only be more bad news. "Hi, Brian. I hope you have some good news for me."

"Actually, I do."

I sit up straighter and rub Sandie behind the ears as she lays her head on my lap.

"Your aunt is no longer contesting the will. Everything is yours." His news should give me a sense of relief, but it makes me feel unsettled.

"Just like that?" I ask, and Brian clears his throat before answering.

"Yes. Her reasoning was false, and after being advised by another solicitor, she withdrew."

"What reasoning?" I want to be happy, but I don't know what I'm really asking. I think to the man in my bed—the one who wants this land. The one who was going to talk with my auntie. He must have, and that's the real reason she withdrew. I wonder now if he paid her off. I wonder if he was sleeping with me to get the land. I tell myself no. I told him the land was his already, only for my aunt who contested the will.

"That, I am unsure of, Siobhan. It could be for a lot of reasons. But it's good news, right?" I don't blame Brian for sounding so unsure. I sound very ungrateful.

"Of course it is. Thanks for letting me know."

"No problem at all. Have you decided what you're doing with the land?" Once again, my mind wanders to the man in my bed. I hope him being here isn't just about the land.

"Not yet," I lie. I don't want a hundred phone calls about land. I just want to digest this bit of information.

After hanging up, I give Sandie a final rub before returning to the bedroom, where I find Finn dressed. He's pulling on a boot when I walk in, and he pauses, looking up at me. My stomach twists, as my thoughts won't slow down and stop with the idea that I'm being used.

"Everything okay?"

It must be written on my face, so I just jump in with both feet. "Did you talk to my aunt?"

He pauses again before he pulls on his boot. Then he answers me. "No, I didn't. Why?" As he looks at me, I can't see any deceit in his eyes, and I relax slightly. I don't know what I was thinking, and even if he had spoken to her, that wasn't such a bad thing. But I can tell he isn't lying.

"She's no longer contesting the will." I still watch him for signs.

"You don't look happy about that."

"I am, I am. It's just... odd. But Brian did say she spoke to a solicitor, and he had advised her against proceeding."

Finn stands up and walks to me. "You should be happy, Siobhan." He takes my arms and gives me a kiss on the cheek, relaxing me further.

"Yeah, I am." I let my stupid worry float away.

"So what are you doing for the rest of the day?" Finn's hands linger on my hips, and I entwine my arms around his neck. I step into the smell of him, and it's so good. My bracelet shines and sparkles as the lights hit it, and it captures my attention. It's really beautiful.

"Thank you so much for my bracelet. It's beautiful," I tell him, looking from the bracelet and then back to his smiling eyes.

"A beautiful bracelet for a beautiful woman."

"You're such a charmer, Finn O'Reagan." I'm smiling—really smiling.

"You're calling me charming again," he says before capturing my lips with his and cutting off the short laugh that threatens to spill from my mouth. His kiss is soft and tender, like he's savoring our final time together. My stomach twists again. I'm not ready to leave him. Maybe he's ready to leave me, though.

When we break the kiss and look at each other, I wonder if I will ever be ready to leave him. It surprises me how quickly I feel so much for him. But there's also the voice in the back of my head that's telling me this is all about land, and once I sell it to him, he'll be gone. Wham, bam, thank you, ma'am.

He hasn't mentioned the land since our last discussion; not since he said he would speak to my aunt. I can't hold his gaze as mixed feelings rush through me, so I focus on my bracelet again.

"What's going through your mind?" he questions, and for the first time with him, I don't want to share my insecurities, because they're about him. So I remove my arms from around his neck and step out of his hold.

"That I have so much to pack before tomorrow," I say instead, giving him a quick glance. His lashes flutter down, not allowing me to see what he's feeling, but I notice a muscle twitch in his jaw.

"Do you want me to give you some space?" He sounds unsure, and his brows furrow.

I wonder if he wants to leave. I'm nodding as I start to gather my clothes off the floor. I don't want to look at him. My heart is pounding out a tune, and my head is screaming at me to tell him not to leave.

CHAPTER THIRTEEN

FINN

MY HEART'S READY TO come out of my chest. I want to leave so badly. Standing in this room with her and knowing what we did to her aunt is torture, but leaving her feels worse. So I stand still as she gathers her clothes. I have so much I want to say, but I can't seem to find the right words.

"Don't leave," I settle on, and she snaps around to face me, her eyes wide.

"What?" She sounds breathless, and I haven't a fucking clue what's going through her mind. Maybe I was a bit of amusement while she was here, but I can't help how I feel about her. I know I can't just walk away and not try to make this work. But what we did to her aunt is eating away at me. I know I should walk away—that secret is huge—but I love her.

"Maybe you could stay longer." I stuff my hands into my pockets to give them something to do. I'm not normally nervous, and I've never asked a girl to stay before, so I'm feeling out of my depth here.

She's clutching her clothes tightly to her chest; the look on her face is conflicted. I want to know what's going through her head. I want to know what she's thinking. "You want me to stay?"

Why does she sound so unsure? Each step I take toward her has her clutching her clothes tighter, and I loosen her hands and remove them, letting the clothing fall to the floor.

"I know we haven't known each other that long, but I'm going to put all my cards on the table, even though my dad told me never to do that." I smile briefly because he would think I was a fool right now. Actually, so would all my brothers. I push my family out of my mind and focus on Siobhan. "I don't want you to go. I want you to stay here with me."

"Here? With you?" The way she says it has me smiling.

"Yes. *Here* with *me*. I think we have something strong here. And I know you feel it too." My heart is pounding, being this honest.

She's in my arms and her lips touch mine. I kiss her back. "I don't want to go either. I want to stay here with you."

My pulse spikes at her words, and my body wants her. The adrenaline from her words has my blood pumping all to one place. I push my body against hers and deepen the kiss, moving us back toward the bed. I have her nightgown off within seconds, and it falls to the floor. My hand goes to the warmth between her legs, and she moans as I easily slip a finger inside. She's as pumped as I am. She makes me feel powerful.

I trail kisses slowly down her jawline, and she throws her head back, offering me her neck, which I kiss. Her moans are growing, and I want nothing more than for her to come in my hand. I move faster as I bend and take one of her nipples in my mouth, sucking it slowly before releasing it. "Oh, God, Finn. I'm going to come!"

I increase my movements as I suck harder on her nipple, and then she releases. Her warm fluid coats my fingers, and it nearly makes *me* come. My jeans have shrunk several sizes, to the point of being painful.

"You're so beautiful," I tell Siobhan as she opens her brown eyes and smiles at me. The bliss on her face makes me feel ten feet tall. Her fingers move to the band of my jeans, and my erection jumps. I need to release.

She opens them and pulls them down, along with my boxers. Looking down at Siobhan on her knees is the best sight I have ever seen in my fucking life, and when she takes me into her mouth, I nearly lose it, but instead, I hold back. I want to savor *every second* of this. Her tongue flicks out, hitting the head, and it jumps again in her mouth, telling me this might actually only be seconds long.

"I can't hold it much longer," I say honestly, and she starts a quick rhythm that has me sinking my hands into her hair as she releases me into her mouth. "Wow." I'm breathless as Siobhan releases me, and when she looks up at me, my heart beats faster. She's everything I could want.

"Give me a moment," she says, leaving the room with her dressing gown. I sit down on the bed until I hear the shower running and decide I could do with a shower too.

The bathroom I walk into is small and made to look even smaller, as it's covered in wooden pine from floor to ceiling. Even the toilet seat is pine; the bathroom hasn't been updated in a long time. My eyes snap to the white shower curtain, and I smile as I pull it back and step in.

"Finn, what are you doing?" With a gasp, Siobhan runs her hand over her face, pushing water away so she can see me.

"I need a wash," I tell her, and she smiles.

"Since you're here, you can wash my back." She hands me a bar of soap, and I grin.

"Let's hope I don't let it drop." She laughs, and it's music to my ears.

"If you drop it, *you* are picking it up," she says once I start to wash her back.

"Oh, you'd like that, would you?"

She glances at me over her shoulder; the grin on her face has my body coming alive again. She turns back around, and I take a moment to admire her perfect backside. She turns around again and speaks. "My back is clean." She has a look in her eyes, one I recognize, and one I would never ignore.

Lathering up the soap, I start with her breasts before making my way down to her sensitive area. "You're a very bad girl, Siobhan," I tell her.

"Then punish me." The answer is unexpected, and I give her what she wants.

CHAPTER FOURTEEN

SIOBHAN

"**S**O ARE YOU STILL interested in buying my land?" I ask Finn as we take Sandie for a walk. It's cold outside, but it always is. The cream jacket I'm wearing has fur on the inside and is waterproof on the outside—perfect for walking in.

Leaves fall from the trees. The orange, green, and yellows are so beautiful. I'm so used to inhaling car fumes in Dublin that the crisp fresh air is nice. It's really nice. It's another reminder of why I don't want to go back to Dublin.

"Are you still willing to sell it?" He kicks a falling twig. The lane is scattered with them. Any kind of wind that blows causes the pass to be coated in leaves and twigs.

"Yes, if the price is right." I glance at him, trying not to smile.

"I feel like you're using me for money." He's teasing; the smirk on his face has my stomach tightening.

"So what am I worth to you, Finn O'Reagan?" We stop walking and stare at each other. His smile slowly fades.

"You are priceless. But the offer of a hundred thousand for the land still stands."

Priceless. I smile at the word. He thinks I'm priceless. He watches me closely.

"That's a crazy amount of money. We should get it valued correctly. I know you're overpaying." And the money sounds nice, but I really don't want to have Finn overpay for it. It just doesn't seem fair.

He removes the few feet between us and pulls me into his arms, surprising me with a kiss to the nose. "You're so moral, and I love that."

The word love has my stomach flipping. I know we aren't fully there yet, but we're so close. Before I can answer, he places a kiss on my lips.

"But take it. It's my father's money, not mine. So take it." He's serious, and I can hear resentment in his voice. I nod as he takes my hand, and we continue walking down the pass. I hope one day he'll tell me his story. I can see he has one to tell.

"Okay. I'll take your father's money," I tell him, and he snorts a laugh. The recent tension leaves, and I'm glad. I hate seeing him upset. It's crazy to care this much for a person in such a short time. But I do.

"How did work take you not going back yet?"

The change in topic has my stomach tightening, and I chew on my lip. I worked so hard to get that job. After taking night courses as I worked in a clothes shop, just to get into a nursing home where I wasn't happy, I continued to take courses and waited until a job came up in the HSE. Then factoring in the time it took to get my Gardaí vetting form—to lose this job wasn't a nice feeling. But leaving Finn was even worse.

"Yeah, they're fine, but I hate not going back. I mean, it's a state job so, you know, it comes with perks that a private nursing home wouldn't provide." We're silent for a few more minutes when we reach the end of the pass. I can see Teresa's house. She lives across the road, her bungalow standing proudly by itself.

"I can put in a word so you can be transferred to Cavan."

I stop walking and pull my jacket tighter around me.

"Are you serious? You could really do that?"

Finn is smiling again. "It would come at a price."

I'm smiling too, my mind going to one place only. "Name your price."

"We could do it in IOUs." Finn takes my hand as we walk back down the pass, and Sandie follows close.

"What kind of IOUs?" I don't actually care; I just love when Finn teases. His blue eyes become so alive, and that cheeky grin does funny things to my stomach.

"Breakfast in bed."

"That's easy," I say.

"Massage my feet."

I laugh a little. "Okay, I could do that."

His lips tug on one side. "You would have to tell me that I'm very well endowed."

I snort a laugh. "You want me to tell you that you're well hung?" I ask incredulously, trying not to giggle.

Now Finn laughs. "You have a way with words, but yes, basically that."

"That's it?" I ask, and his eyes darken.

"Not even close."

"You want to cash in on your IOUs?" I ask as everything starts to tingle, and I wonder how I could do it again, but I can. With Finn, I can.

"I would like that very much." His serious tone has me walking faster to the house.

"You better live up to your word, Finn," I tell him, and he tugs on my hand.

"Consider the job in Cavan yours."

I haven't a clue if he's serious or not, but the idea that it might be remotely possible marks today as the best day of my life, and as we enter my house, I know this will be the cherry on top.

CHAPTER FIFTEEN

FINN

I DON'T KNOW WHY I'm hesitating outside the dining room. My dad is in there alone, so this is the perfect opportunity to talk to him.

After leaving Siobhan's, I got Shane to call in a favor at the hospital, making sure Siobhan has a job to start in the next few weeks. When I rang her, she was on cloud nine, and my heart squeezed with pride that I had done that. Shane didn't ask any questions; he did it for me without hesitation. Him doing it so easily had me wanting to back away, but it was worth it. No doubt I would owe him in the future, but for Siobhan, I didn't mind. I suppose our family could be useful at times, though I didn't know what Shane had to do to call in the favor.

I knew Liam was the one who had spoken to Brian Harris; he took care of any official business like that. A stuffed envelope was never passed up, and as much as I hated the bullshit of politics, I was glad for it now.

I have one last thing to do, and that's to tell my dad that the land is ours. I wanted him to be proud of me, but now... I don't know. It's Siobhan's land, and I just don't feel that way anymore.

"If you want to speak with him alone, I'll wait five more minutes." Liam speaks from behind me, and I turn to see him in a new suit, his eyes skimming over me like he doesn't actually see me. His brown eyes are almost black, and I wonder about the saying that the eyes are the door to the soul. If it's true, his soul is a very dark place.

"Yeah, thanks," I tell him and go into the dining room. My father doesn't look up from a file in front of him. He keeps flicking until I'm close enough to see. It's then that he closes it.

"Finn, your week is almost up," he tells me with a gleam in his eyes, one that warns me not to disappoint him.

"We have the land."

He doesn't smile just nods. "Good. Now don't forget we're all having dinner here tonight."

I groan internally. I completely forgot. We celebrate the anniversary of our mother's death every year by all coming together and having a meal. It's painful, and I hate it.

"Of course. I can't wait," I tell him, and he gives me a second nod. He's not one to show too much emotion, but his nods are a really good sign and would normally have me feeling ten feet tall, but now the only person who seems to have that power over me is Siobhan. Maybe I should be grateful to my father—if only for him wanting the land. Otherwise, I never would have met Siobhan.

I leave as he returns to his file, and I pass Liam as he goes in. I used to wonder what they got up to, but as I grew older, the thoughts of being involved in their meetings made me uncomfortable. The depth of criminal activity they're involved in is far too deep for me. I often think that me and Darragh only ever see the surface.

"What's the jazz?" Darragh arrives at the front door, and he doesn't look hungover. This is a surprise.

"We have the family meal tonight." That gets a string of curses from Darragh, and I smile at how inventive he is.

I go into the kitchen to get a bowl of cereal; Mary isn't in today. I'm not sure why, but I want one of her turkey and cranberry sandwiches that she makes with the most perfect stuffing. But cornflakes will have to do. Darragh follows me in and pours himself a bowl. He's like a pig at a trough as he eats. Milk drips down his chin, and his noises are loud and disgusting.

"You're turning my fucking stomach," I tell him while shifting in my seat so I don't have to look at his slobbering face.

"What's wrong with you?" he asks. His mouth is full of cereal, so I don't answer. "Ah, you got blue balls."

Now I glance at him. "Why is everything about sex with you?" I shake my head. I know he's prodding me to see if I'll spill, but I won't.

"There are four things that are everything to me." Darragh holds up his spoon. "One is sex." He grins, and I continue to eat my cereal, not really caring what the other three are, but he wants to share. "The second is money, third partying, and last family."

I snort. "In that order?"

He actually thinks about it. "Yes, but hold up. So the four Ps—partying, pounds, pussy, and papa."

Sometimes I want to deck him. He starts rhyming it off again, trying to sing when Shane walks in.

"You're a jackass," I tell him as I place my bowl in the sink.

"I'm with Finn on this," Shane says, but he's grinning at Darragh. It's odd to see Shane smiling, and I don't ruin the moment with morbid thoughts.

"Okay, fine, what about the four Fs?" Darragh continues. I'm a glutton for punishment and actually wait to hear how he will rhyme this off. "Family, fun times, the fifties and fannies." I'm laughing when I shouldn't, but it's so bad that it's funny.

"Don't start singing that at the table today," Shane says, sobering up the room. He goes to the fridge with no idea of the change in atmosphere. He's like Liam in ways—they don't seem to understand human emotion or the impact their words have. I can only hope the meal is quick and quiet.

Dad sits at the head of the table with Shane to his left and Liam to his right. I sit beside Liam and across from Darragh, who's playing with his peas. One bounces across the table, and we all focus on it. I gulp my wine. It isn't always like this. Once, this table was filled with laughter, but we've lost too much.

Father raises his glass. "To family. *An clann.*" He says the English and the Irish of it, and we all repeat his words as we drink. I look at Darragh; his glass is empty, so he's sucking in air. He looks across at me and winks before his foot connects with my leg. I don't shout out like I want to, as Dad isn't finished speaking.

"I have allowed Connor his vacations many times." He says this with a wave of his hand, but my heart races. "This one has been the longest and I'm ready for him to return home."

I want to see Connor so bad, and I'm angry at him for leaving, but the thoughts of him being dragged back here isn't fair. He deserves to find his happiness, and I know he will never find it in this place.

"You know where he is?" I ask. The stillness around the table tells me I'm not the only one who's been impacted by my father's words.

"He has a job, a place to stay. A friend of mine is keeping an eye on him. But I want him home." Father's words are said as he looks at each of us. When he looks at me, I speak up.

"I'll go," I say. I'm angry at Connor for leaving, but to have him back would complete me. Especially after finding Siobhan. God, he would really like her. I know wanting him back is selfish, but I'm no angel.

"No." My father turns to Shane. "I want *you* to bring Connor home." Shane nods and raises his glass. We all follow suit.

I look at Darragh, and he's no longer messing around. I hate that Shane is the one to get picked again. He always gets picked. He doesn't even get on with Connor, but Shane will bring him home.

If I went, my heart might overrule my head, and I might tell Connor he doesn't have to come. Maybe Father sees that weakness in me. Does it matter who brings Connor home? The fact he's coming home is the important part.

"To Connor," Darragh says, and I find myself smiling. I'm about to get my brother back.

"To Connor," we all repeat, except for Father. He does raise his glass, but he never toasts to Connor.

***

CONTINUE READING THE O'REAGAN BROTHERS WITH VICIOUS – A FULL LENGTH NOVEL for only .99c HERE

Killing for me is easy. Loving is an entirely different thing.

Una is the only person I ever gave a damn about, but she's off limits. I'm grateful she only spends the summer with us. I can't risk her getting involved in my life of crime. But now she's here, all grown up, and this time, I don't think I can stay away from her.

When Una starts partying with Darragh, who's as wild and unpredictable as they come, I can't afford keeping my distance any longer. Bodies seem to stack up wherever he goes. Cleaning up his messes used to be annoying. Now I have Una to consider, Una to protect.

My family is belly deep in the criminal underworld, and she's a distraction I can't afford. The closer she gets to me, the more I'm spiraling out of control.

I can't let her see who I really am, but I can't seem to let her go.

Start Reading Vicious for a fast-paced, suspenseful read today!
https://www.authorvicarter.com/books/the-wild-irish-series/vicious-1

About The Author

When Vi Carter isn't writing contemporary & dark romance books, that feature the mafia, are filled with suspense, and take you on a fast paced ride, you can find her reading her favorite authors, baking, taking photos or watching Netflix. Married with three children, Vi divides her time between motherhood and all the other hats she wears as an Author. She has declared herself a coffee & chocolate addict! Do not judge
Social Media Links for Vi Carter
www.authorvicarter.com

www.ingramcontent.com/pod-product-compliance
Lightning Source LLC
Chambersburg PA
CBHW030810190726
48285CB00003B/1106